V CARD

A DARK NOVELLA

SYBIL KNIGHT

COVER CREATOR: ARTISTA GRÁFICO
EDITING: KAT PAGAN, PAGAN PROOFREADING
FORMATTING: DAHLIA REIGN LLC

SOCIALS:

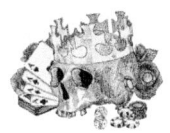

EMAIL: AUTHORSYBILKNIGHT@GMAIL.COM

NEWSLETTER: WWW.SENDFOX.COM/DAHLIAANDSYBIL

FACEBOOK GROUP:
WWW.FACEBOOK.COM/GROUPS/DAHLIAANDSYBILSLIT-
TEDEVILS

INSTAGRAM:
WWW.INSTRAGRAM.COM/AUTHOR.SYBIL.KNIGHT

FACEBOOK PAGE:
WWW.FACEBOOK.COM/AUTHORSYBILKNIGHT

TIKTOK: WWW.TIKTOK.COM/@QUEENSOFCHAOSBOOKS

♦♠♥♣♦♠♥♣♦

DEDICATION

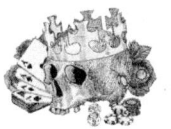

*To anyone and everyone
who's ever wanted a do-over,
this one's for you!*

♦♠♥♣♦♠♥♣♦

TRIGGER WARNING:

THE AUTHOR ASKS THAT YOU HEED THE FOLLOWING LIST OF POTENTIAL TRIGGERS:

- OVERALL SEXUALLY EXPLICIT CONTENT
- AGE-GAP (BOTH ADULTS)
- VIRGIN TROPE
- CNC/DUBCON
- IMBALANCE OF POWER
- GAMBLING ADDICTION
- TOBACCO USE
- COERCION
- FORCED PROXIMITY/CONFINEMENT
- AND MORE...

AUTHOR NOTES:

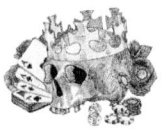

LOOK. I'M GONNA BE STRAIGHT UP WITH YOU.
THIS STORY IS SUPER SHORT AND SUPER SPICY.
I'M TALKING LIKE 90% SMUT HERE.
THERE IS A PLOT THOUGH!
YOU JUST HAVE TO WEAVE YOUR WAY THROUGH A
WHOLE LOT OF DICK IN HOLES TO GET THERE.

ARE YOU READY?
ARE YOU READY FOR ALL THAT DICK IN HOLES?
OKAY THEN, LET'S GO... JUST WATCH WHERE YOU SIT.
(THOSE AREN'T YOGURT STAINS.)

♦♠♥♣♦♠♥♣♦

BLURB:

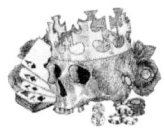

THE STAKES WERE HIGH. HIS BODY COUNT WAS HIGHER.

THE LADIES LOVED ME. BOTH THE ONES I SHOVED OUT MY HOTEL ROOM DOOR EVERY MORNING *AND* THE ONES I WAS CURRENTLY FLICKING BETWEEN MY THUMBS. A PAIR OF QUEENS. MY IDEAL THREESOME.

BUT THESE GALS WERE FICKLE, WHEREAS LADY LUCK WAS THE TYPE TO NEVER LEAVE MY SIDE. IT WAS THE SAME REASON THE GIRL SITTING ACROSS FROM ME NEVER STOOD A CHANCE.

COULDN'T BLAME HER. NOT REALLY. PRETTY LITTLE THING DIDN'T KNOW SHE WAS TREADING IN SHARK-INFESTED WATERS. OR THAT THE ONLY CARD SHE HAD LEFT AT HER DISPOSAL... JUST SO HAPPENED TO BE MY FAVORITE ONE TO TAKE. TAKING WASN'T THE ONLY

THING I DID THOUGH. I WAS A GIVER TOO. DEMANDS, DEGRADATION, DIC—

WELL, I THINK YOU CATCH MY DRIFT. POINT WAS, THE MOMENT SHE DECIDED TO GO ALL-IN WAS THE EXACT MOMENT SHE AGREED TO LET ME DO THE SAME.

GAME ON, BABY GIRL.

◆♠♥♣◆♠♥♣◆

PROLOGUE

"Your call, sweetheart." I grinned. Watching as a pair of honey-colored eyes peered up at me, then immediately dropped back down to the hand she was clutching a little too tight between a set of manicured fingertips. This particular kitten had pretty pink claws that were two-sizes too big for her.

I shook my head. *And if she wasn't careful, I was gonna have to demand a new deck.* No way in hell was I about to chance someone marking a perfectly good stack of cards. Didn't matter if that shit was intentional or an honest mistake. She hadn't been on this earth long enough to know what was good for her, and I'd been on it too long to let a little girl get the slip on me.

I might not have known her, might not have ever seen her before tonight, but I sure as shit knew her type. I'd clocked her the moment she started rounding the room before deciding I was the chump she was gonna try to distract with one palm on his thigh and another creeping into his wallet. She was used to a bunch of limp dicks letting her win—or at the very least, she was used to throwing them off their game. Because *hers* was shit.

It wouldn't take more than a few rounds for the kid to realize she'd chosen poorly. I wasn't her meal ticket. I wasn't easily distracted either. I might have allowed myself a peek at her tits, but it was the rest of her I was more interested in. It was the rest of her that told me everything I needed to know.

All I had to do was read her facial expressions. Study her mannerisms. Listen for the little sounds she made after each hand was dealt. That's what happened when you were young and your poker face was nonexistent. You were an open book for fuckers like me, the kind of guy who knew better than to drink when he was working a table.

A slurping sound had my glare sweeping over the fruity cocktail the kitten was nursing through one of those straws with the loops in it. Her third since slinking her way into that seat with the confidence of a betta fish that had never seen outside its bowl. And I had to keep from rolling my eyes. Another novice move. You didn't need your senses dulled by alcohol. You needed them sharpened by years of practice.

Unlike the crowds that flocked to the money pits, lured by all that glitter and gold, I had no problem tuning it out. The other players and the environment built brick by brick to distract you. My sole focus glued to the cards in my hand and the chips in front of me. The noise melted away. The lights didn't matter. Even the smoke seemed to clear until all I could think about was the offer that hung between us. Her virginity in exchange for another stack of chips. Unless she happened to be staring at an ace of diamonds.

The sudden droop of those plump, overly-painted lips told me she wasn't, though. Not that it seemed to affect her willingness to bluff. The girl didn't say a word as she tossed her remaining chips into the pot. *All-in.*

It was a bold move for someone whose feet barely touched the floor without the help of those ridiculous heels. She probably thought the shoes and makeup made her look older. They didn't. They made her look like she was trying too hard. A bright-red target for those of us circling the casino room floors as soon as we tasted fresh blood in the water.

I lifted a challenging brow, calling her bluff before the poor kid even realized her mistake as I flipped my hand over on the table. A pair of queens to her jack and king.

Her jaw dropped, her mouth opening and closing a few times like one of those little molly fish with the big bug eyes. She was just as colorful too, in that emerald green evening gown that left little to the imagination when it came to what was underneath it.

I could see the wheels turning in her head, and quickly cut off whatever argument she was planning with a *tsk* of my tongue before gesturing for security to come and collect my winnings. Which tonight included the girl in front of me and whatever she was hiding between those thighs I could see her clenching from all the way over here.

CHAPTER ONE

This was just physical. It wasn't about romance or whatever crazy ideas the chicks I brought upstairs got in their minds when I agreed to bury my face in their cunts for a couple of hours. It was one of the very few downsides to fucking around with virgins. They thought going home smelling like my cum was as good as a marriage proposal. When all it really was, was an exchange of bodily fluids. A stress-reliever. Something that helped me relax after a long night sitting in a hard seat when I had no choice but to keep my urges at bay.

But here, in this room, I could let loose as much as I could maintain control. It was my favorite balancing act. Seeing how far I could test my own limits before allowing myself to give in to them.

It didn't really matter what they looked like, the

women I allowed the privilege of feeling my dick sinking deep into their cunts. The ones who got the literal pleasure of having my tongue swirl around their clits until they were screaming a stranger's name. All I cared about was that I was the first one to do it. Because I was an only child, a selfish son of a bitch who never learned to share.

I wasn't about to apologize for that. You didn't have to like me to fuck me. And I sure as shit didn't have to like you either. That was the very definition of hate sex, after all.

It wasn't until we were tucked away in the sanctity of my executive suite, far from the busy Vegas streets below us and all the lurking eyes lingering there, that I was able to fully appreciate tonight's entertainment. And I had to admit without all the flashing lights and noise, without the outside distractions, the girl was more than a bit pleasing to the eye.

She was pretty. With an hourglass silhouette that hinted at the curves she was hiding as she folded in on herself. Her arms crossed over her chest and her weight shifting from foot to foot.

I took a step forward, my hands clasped behind my back as I assessed the little molly who hadn't realized she wasn't the bait. She was the main course. Scanned her from head to fucking toe and memorized everything between. Every freckle, scar, beauty mark. The way her auburn hair had flecks of red in it and curled at the ends. How her pale skin and tight-fitting gown made her eyes pop. Her long lashes framing those same eyes as they stared up at me before dropping back down to her toes. I'd made her remove her heels as well as the several layers of lipstick she had caked on her mouth.

I wanted her natural and... *unencumbered* for everything I had planned for her.

I stepped aside to get a sense of her true height now that she wasn't using those sparkly shoes as a crutch and looked her over once more. From a different angle. She was a petite little thing. Barely five-foot to my six... something. I didn't need to pull out a ruler to get exacts. I was big, much bigger than she was, and that was all that mattered. I intimidated her without having to do a thing but stand upright.

My gaze flicked to her cleavage, and I took notice of how shallow her breaths were, her chest heaving as the air was sucked in and forced out again. How her skin was pebbled even though I hadn't lifted a hand to touch her yet. She was scared. And she should be. She'd offered herself up to a stranger, a man who had the means to ensure she'd never leave this room if I didn't want her to leave it. Had the methods to ensure she was never found again unless I wanted her found.

I could do that, but it wasn't my intention. If she had chosen to sit at someone else's table, she might not have been so lucky though. And she could be going home wrapped up in a body bag, instead of the designer label I had yet to peel back—the same one that she'd be wearing when I shipped her out in a few hours.

That part was coming. Not long after I did. But I had no desire to rush the process.

Despite the fear I could feel radiating off her, the slight sheer of perspiration I could make out on her forehead, I didn't look at this girl like a predator would its prey. No, my appraisal was more refined than animalistic.

She was a delicacy and I was the kind of guy who enjoyed a good meal. I didn't fuck. I didn't make love either. I indulged in flesh. Consumed it. Worshiped the act like a dying man praying for his salvation. It meant the difference between fingerpainting and swiping the last brushstroke on a masterpiece. Between banging a few keys and conducting a symphony. An apprentice and a master of the arts. *Someone who liked to play Uno and a professional card shark.*

So, yeah, I eyed the girl how an accomplished violinist would examine a commissioned instrument. How taut the strings. How long the neck. How curvaceous the waist. It all fell to my judgmental gaze.

"You can lose the dress now," I instructed as I shifted the material from her shoulders, watching it flutter down her body before pooling at her feet. The satisfaction of my grin meeting the terror of her eyes.

She was clean. Unmarked. No open sores or indications to suggest her claims weren't true. Which meant she would do.

At least for tonight. After that, her spending habits and piss-poor game play were someone else's problem.

CHAPTER TWO

"Your name." It was a command. Not a question. Or a request.

When the girl didn't immediately respond, choosing to stare at her matching pink pedicure instead of doing what she was told, my arm shot forward and my index finger snapped her chin towards the ceiling. Until my narrowed glare met the fluttering of those long, thick lashes she'd spent far too much time dolling up and fanning out just to have them covered in my cum a short few hours later.

I grinned at the thought, quickly shoving my amusement aside before it accidentally slipped free. We had a lot of work to do, only a few hours to do it, and one of us was acting a little bratty at the moment.

It would be a shame if she had to learn the hard

way. It meant sacrificing her own enjoyment for mine. Because ticking clock or not, I didn't repeat myself. I wouldn't. The weight of my presence was more than enough to bend someone to my will. Especially this particular someone. Seeing as my little molly fish looked more like a *deer in headlights* now that she was standing in front of me.

"Rose," she stammered out while licking at her dry lips. A sign of her growing distress.

"Your full name." It didn't matter. I wouldn't remember it. But it wasn't about that. It was about dominating the exchange. About absolute compliance. About having her submit to me without physically forcing her to do it.

"R-Rosalind."

Okay, well, that wasn't what I asked. I'd asked for her full name. She was still scared though. Likely not thinking straight with all the blood rushing between her legs and making her lightheaded on her feet. So I'd let that one slide.

I didn't move as I continued to watch her. Didn't show approval or voice dissatisfaction. My expression remained neutral. Unforgiving. This was a dance, and the girl was meant to follow my lead. Not the other way around.

"Age," I tossed out another command as I turned my back to her and began loosening my tie. Fucking thing was strangling me, and not in the way either of us would enjoy.

"Old enough." Her voice was louder this time. It also sounded a little annoyed. *That* wouldn't do.

But once again, I refused to repeat myself. Instead, I spun in her direction and slowly craned my neck, allowing my gaze to travel from the ceiling above her head and drop to her face before searing into a pair of rapidly-widening pupils.

"Twenty-three," she whispered.

I maintained eye contact until all the color was drained from her cheeks and I was staring into two panicked black holes. Each reflecting my silhouette while that honey hue was reduced to a matching set of those flimsy stacking rings the cocktail waitresses liked to wear. Flashy enough to catch the light but missing all the sparkle. I didn't want flashy. I wanted the flames of lust. So overbearing it consumed her.

"Nineteen," the girl quickly corrected herself.

I paused before accepting that answer as truth (or something close to it) and began removing my cuff links. Placing them neatly on the dresser before returning my attention to my tie. By the time I spun back to the girl, my hands were tucked into my pockets and my shirt was hanging open.

I knew I looked good. I also knew my friend here appreciated the view. It was an egotistical thought to have about yourself. But I was the type who relied on facts. Not opinions. And *the fact* was I'd spent more hours than I cared to count focused on perfecting a body that might as well have been a fine wine. Because it only got better and *more defined* with age.

The girl didn't breathe. She didn't dare. She didn't move either, likely too afraid to do much of anything. But it wasn't her fear I sought; it was her obedience. The breaking of her will when she finally understood it was best for both of us.

"The bed." Two words. So many possibilities. But at the moment, I only wanted to position her there.

Seeming to grasp my meaning, the girl stepped away until the underside of her knees clipped the mattress's edge. Then she shuffled back, her eyes locked on mine as she centered herself in the middle of the king-sized comforter. An unwrapped present. Pristine packaging waiting to be enjoyed.

I watched her for another moment, wondering whether she would resign herself to her fate or try to weasel her way out of it.

Fortunately for her, I didn't have to wonder for long. Because no more than a few seconds ticked by before acceptance stared back at me.

Good girl. The praise danced around in my head but I wouldn't give it to her just yet. She hadn't earned it. Baby steps and all that.

CHAPTER THREE

I allowed the silence to stretch on between us. I didn't question her again, and she seemed to pick up on the fact she shouldn't ask anything herself.

It made her uncomfortable, though. It quickened her pulse. Sent surges of anxiety-induced adrenaline coursing through those veins of hers. I could see them throbbing in her throat. Could already imagine my fingertips gripping just under her chin, holding that quivering band of muscle in place while restricting her air supply. She wouldn't know what to make of it. Whether she liked it or feared me. Teetering on the edge of both before succumbing to the pleasure I would give her.

I cracked my neck, anchoring myself to the present instead of all the delicious possibilities the future held. And watched her watching me. The left side of my mouth creased into an almost-smirk. Just barely there. "I won't lie to you, baby girl. This is gonna hurt. But then it won't and you'll hardly remember a time when it did."

She mumbled a response. But I had impeccable hearing and perfect 20/20 vision. Which meant there was no hiding the way her lips parted and twisted on a sneer.

"I didn't catch that... Say it again." I took the two steps that brought me to the edge of the mattress and slid up the bed before she realized I was even moving. "Louder this time."

Defiance. I saw a glimmer of it. It twinkled in her eyes. Youth did that to you. Innocence too. Sparked a sense of invincibility that life sought to extinguish. It never lasted long and I knew it wouldn't last long here either.

"I said... why virgins? Why do you like virgins?" She was trying to understand me. Or perhaps just stall the inevitable...

Didn't matter which it was. This thing between us was only temporary. And then she'd be on her way. Out my door and on her ass. She'd given me her word and I didn't take kindly to those who didn't make good on their promises.

"Why do I like virgins? Why does anyone like anything?" I shrugged a single shoulder, deciding to indulge the girl for a moment. Though I had no idea why I was bothering. Boredom maybe. "It's a preference, an acquired taste. Like the first bite of veal served at the ideal temperature. Tender and expertly seasoned... There's just something about knowing it's both delicious *and* wrong that has your mouth watering..."

I leaned forward and flicked my tongue across her lips.

"Your pants stretching..."

I wrenched her arm away from her side and forced her to grip my cock through the layers of fabric between us. A slight grin tipped up my face as I squeezed once, my palm guiding hers before I quickly dropped her hand back onto the bed. Watching her stare down at her fingertips like I'd somehow burned her. Then I lowered my mouth to her ear again.

"Your pupils dilating." This had my grin widening as her eyes seemed to follow my command without her brain realizing she was doing it. "It's not about the poor innocent calf. It's about your body's instinctual reaction to that pink juice dripping onto a fresh white linen. How that being's sole purpose is to be born, thrive, and wait to bring you pleasure. Before you move on to the next one."

"So, you're saying I'm no better than a piece of meat? Livestock? *A bloated baby cow?*" she huffed, and my nostrils flared as I suppressed my laughter. She was insulted when she should be grateful.

This wasn't a punishment. It was an opportunity. For each of us. Just in a slightly different way.

"Oh no, sweetheart, you're missing the point. You aren't just a meal. You're an *experience*. Something meant to be enjoyed in the moment, over an extended period of time, but never dwelled on. And that's the difference between a drive-through cheese-burger and a gourmet spread."

On the last word, I gripped the girl's ankles. Tugged her forward and yanked her legs apart. Her slight gasp sent a jolt from my fingertips digging into her skin straight to my cock.

I took a deep breath, forcing the pounding in my chest to even out as the thrill of the chase tried to do the opposite. It was hard to maintain your composure when your favorite meal was laid out in front of you, no matter how well-practiced you were at doing it.

I lowered my face to her body, gliding my flattened tongue from the sensitive flesh just above her knee up the seams of her thigh, pausing at the juncture of where her leg met her pelvic bone before pulling back to savor the way her sweat danced across my tastebuds. Once it dissipated, no more than a distant memory, I grasped each of her wrists in one of my hands and wrenched them above her head. My control hanging on by a loose thread as I stretched her out in front of me.

I paused for a moment, appreciating the erotic

display like an artist trying to determine if this stroke was his first or his last, before I wrapped her fingers around the fabric of the bedsheet until she clutched a handful in each tiny, unblemished fist. Then I leaned forward, my mouth a breath away from her lips. "Your wrists are locked to that spot."

She glanced up, the question bouncing around in her head evident in the slight crease of her brow and craning of her neck as she tried to see what I was doing.

"Not literally, of course. But for all intents and purposes, they are. I'm not a fan of physical restraints—they're..." My gaze drifted upwards, as if the ceiling held the answer, as I searched for the best way to explain my reasoning to someone who didn't see the world like I did. And probably never could. "...tactless. Requiring such minimal skill set." Then my eyes dropped back to the woman beneath me as I breathed my next words into the shell of her ear. "You will not move because I'm telling you not to move. Not because an object outside my control makes it impossible to do. And not because you're deprived of the option. Do you understand?"

The girl nodded. The action was slight. Just a quick dip of her chin down and up again. Barely discernible to anyone who wasn't looking but present nonetheless.

"Good girl," I hummed as if the two words were instrumental, my left hand traveling down the base of her throat, over the mound of her breast, along the slight protrusion of each of her ribs before thrumming against her hip and slipping away to push myself off the mattress and onto my feet. "I'll be back."

I didn't repeat my instructions. But they hung in the air without me having to say them. *Do not move. Or you will not like the consequences, little molly.*

CHAPTER FOUR

I watched her for an hour, my ass firmly planted in the chair and my camera angled so that the outline of her body was in its sights, and started to wonder if the screen had frozen. A quick slap against the side of the monitor told me shit was working just fine, though.

The girl lay motionless on the bed. Other than the gentle rise and fall of her breasts—the only visible proof of life she offered whoever cared enough to be looking—she appeared the perfect image of self-discipline. I hadn't told her how long I'd be. That was part of the test of wills. The game I enjoyed when it came to breaking them. And I didn't know what to make of her, whether I'd found the ideal submissive or the girl who'd break me instead.

Both possibilities sent a chill down my spine. I was growing impatient, another emotion I wasn't used to dealing with. I enjoyed delayed gratification as much as the next guy. Most of the time anyway. And right now, *this delay* was meant to aggravate her, not me.

Instead, she lay there in comfortable silence— like some Disney princess just waiting for her white knight to kiss her stupid—while I paced the adjoining room like a canine in heat. My hands raking through my meticulously combed hair and digging into the flesh of my scalp.

The slight sting centered me, deadened the unease crawling up the back of my neck and whispering in my ear. Until my gaze zeroed in on the girl on the screen. The girl who seemed to stare back at me through the glass. No, not at... *through*. Her eyes searing into me. As if she *saw* me.

She couldn't, of course, and I knew it was my mind playing tricks on me... yet I couldn't quite figure out what about her was so unnerving. She was like all the others before her. She smelled the same, tasted the same. Her porcelain skin even felt the same. Untouched. Supple, like that veal I was already picturing. And pink.

However, there was something different about her eyes and the way she looked at me. Almost as though she were dissecting me from the inside out. They were innocent, yes, bright and shiny and so very naïve. But beyond that, there was more...

I powered off the screen, yanking my shirt from

my shoulders and jerking my belt from its loops before tossing both onto the floor. Then I stalked back into view of the girl with the dark, haunting eyes. There was a hint of green to them but only in the right light. Why I knew that, I wasn't sure. Didn't make the observation any less true, though.

She watched me enter the room, approach her, but she didn't move. Her stillness to the point of unsettling. Even as her neck slowly pivoted to follow my path to the edge of the bed. Like one of those creepy animatronic dolls in an abandoned funhouse suddenly coming back to life and staring at you.

I unbuttoned my fly and drew the zipper down to its base, my focus on the girl as I stepped out of my pants and kicked them aside. Any other time, I'd remove each article of clothing smoothly before carefully draping it over the side chair, with the kind of precision I used whenever I was playing my hand at the card table. My every action was meant to be refined, controlled, purposeful. But today, my instincts were raw. More primal than restrained.

That didn't mean I was inclined to rush. *I wouldn't rush.* I never rushed. You didn't rush what was meant to be appreciated. That said, something kept me from being able to follow my usual routine.

I removed my boxers in a similar fashion, a slow reveal before chucking them onto the floor. My cock moistened at the tip, prepared to lay waste to the pounds of flesh splayed out in front of me. I resisted the urge to reach down and stroke myself, to relieve some of the tension that had built up over the last hour or so. Longer, seeing as this girl had been testing my willpower since the moment she thought *my* money was *her* fair game.

My palms itched by my sides and my pelvic muscles twitched with the surge of blood flow. But instead of giving in, I climbed up her body, shifting her thighs to each side and resting my tip mere centimeters from her needy cunt. Then I released her hands from their grip on the sheet. The gesture was sensual, nearly affectionate as I plucked them away, a finger at a time, and massaged each pink kitten claw from base to nail, stimulating her nerve endings and returning her circulation.

And not because I cared. But because I wanted her to feel everything I was about to do to her. She might have looked like a doll but that didn't mean I wanted to fuck one. I liked my women inexperienced. Not dead.

CHAPTER FIVE

It'd taken years of practice. Hours of nearly edging myself to get to this point. Where I could be so close to the end game without going all-in. Poker didn't just teach you patience. It taught you how much sweeter the pot could be if you were just willing to wait for it.

That practice was just as easily put into play here. In the bedroom. When coming wasn't as pleasurable as all the steps that it took you to get there. Each little whimper I elicited was like an appetizer, offering me a taste of what the main course would be. The thing was, I wasn't interested in digging in just yet. Not when there was so much more to savor.

I brushed the tip of my finger over her clit and watched the way the girl shuddered beneath me, those little bundles of nerves begging for all the sensations her body had never experienced before.

It didn't matter how many times I'd seen it. It always amazed me. How instinctual it was to seek out the stimulation. Humans were born and bred to fuck. Whether or not it resulted in procreation was of little consequence. We were selfish creatures. Far more focused on our own enjoyment than ensuring the species' survival. And women weren't any less guilty than men. They just hid it better. Because society told them they needed to.

Deep down, they wanted this as much as we did. They wanted to be fucked and used and left in a pool of mixed bodily fluids. It was what drew them to me. What brought this girl to my table when there were so many others to choose from.

The prey recognized the predator. And this little piece of unplucked fruit wanted to be chewed up and swallowed. She wanted all the dirty things I planned to do to her.

That first swipe of my tongue up her center told me I was right, while the way she tried not to buck beneath me confirmed this was as new to her as her taste was to me.

Experienced women leaned into you, met you thrust for thrust in a practiced rhythm they'd learned over the years. Using their hips to guide you this way or that. Because they knew how they liked it. How to get from point A to point B without any of the fumbling they were forced to endure between—

from the type of men who didn't know what they were doing.

I didn't enjoy a girl who knew what she wanted. I enjoyed showing her what she needed. How much better it could be when we took our time. I didn't want to retrain a saddled mare. I wanted to break in that new foal.

Did that make me selfish? Maybe. Then again, the way they cried out my name that first time—how their bodies gave in to that first internal orgasm because there was a fucking difference—suggested I was a giver by nature. And these girls were lucky to be on the receiving end.

She was scared. Her prickled skin speaking to her natural instincts to appear more intimidating while her shallow breaths were meant to keep her hidden from view. The perfect example of fight or flight working in tandem.

It made her taste both sweet and salty, a hint of soap burning the tip of my tongue as I dragged it just above where she needed me most. Where I could feel that ache building in her lower stomach as I pressed two fingers on top of that spot I could find with my eyes closed and applied the slightest hint of pressure.

She tensed—they always did, so unfamiliar with their own bodies they couldn't discern the difference between pain and pleasure—before she melted against the mattress. So agonizingly wound up and relaxed at the same time as I inhaled her scent deep into my lungs.

The next lap of my tongue started at the apex of her left thigh, slowly trailing its way across her smooth skin, over to the right in a zigzag motion that had her squirming against the bed.

"You move," I warned between clenched teeth. "I stop moving. And I promise you it'll be much better for both of us if I warm you up first."

Her only response was a whimper. Not exactly the compliance I was looking for. But for once in my life, I was too fucking worked up to follow through on my threat. Instead, I dove in face-first until I was up to my nose in her juices while mine leaked through the sheets and onto the mattress. Like I was some teenager who didn't know how to keep from coming in his pants.

What the fuck.

CHAPTER SIX

S heer stubbornness had me clutching her thighs in each of my palms and dragging her down the mattress until I was kneeling on the floor, her ass teetering on the edge of the bed as I spread her pussy lips so far apart and open for me I could practically see inside her. Each time she tried to shoot back up or reach out and grab on to me, I stopped moving. Pressing a palm on her sternum and shoving her against the sheets again.

I'd tell her when I was done. And I wasn't done.

This was for me as much as it was for her. I enjoyed the taste, the smell, being the first to dive into unexplored territory and stake my claim for every man who came after me. There would be others. I didn't indulge repeat customers. But none of them would ever live up to the permanent mark

I'd leave in my wake. The ghost of my touch, the memory of my cock splitting them in two and leaving them in pieces for someone else to clean up and try to put back together.

Another observation that was more fact than opinion.

I knew what I could do. What I did. What I was currently doing with the arousal that was quickly pooling between her thighs. It was the kind of thing that couldn't be faked. The body's natural reaction to everything I did to it. Each new sensation I brought to the surface and sent rushing through her like a wave of ecstasy.

It fascinated me. The expressions she made. The way her brows creased, how her eyelashes fluttered as she struggled to decide if she wanted to pry them open or squeeze them shut. The curiosity and confusion. The thrill and euphoria. Like all that build up before the first drop of a roller coaster—the juddering of the cart, the clicking of the tracks and tension of the cables. The fear of the unknown. It was never the same after that. Not after you knew what to expect.

I waited for her to come down from her second external orgasm before I crawled back over her and got into position. The moment my cock slipped through that first ring of muscle, just the tip testing the waters, her arms shot out. Her palms closing over my wrists like a little resistance was enough to stop me. It wasn't.

My pause had nothing to do with her sudden reluctance, and everything to do with the fact I had no intention of diving all the way into the pool just yet.

CHAPTER SEVEN

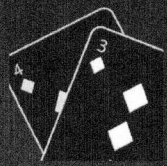

"What are you doing?" she gasped, the way her brows creased in the middle giving her an added innocence that made my dick that much harder as I struggled to keep it in check.

Using one arm to support my full weight, I lifted the other, gesturing between us as I gave the girl an unobstructed view of where our bodies were just barely connected. "Need a little sex education, baby girl? The school system really did fail you, huh?" I grunted, because it was difficult to speak when all the blood meant for my brain was rushing downward at a rate that left my IQ significantly lower than usual.

She shook her head from side to side. "No, I mean aren't you going to use... you know?"

I lifted a questioning brow. *Because, no, I didn't know.*

"Protection—"

I barked out a laugh before the ridiculous word had time to fully form in her mouth. "I fuck virgins, sweetheart. Doesn't get cleaner than that. And if you're worried about getting knocked up, don't. I've been shooting blanks for the last ten years."

Getting snipped was one of the best decisions I'd made. It was far easier than forcing a morning-after pill down a chick's throat and keeping your fingers crossed it stayed there. I had too much to lose to risk being saddled by some teenager who assumed having my bastard would also have her all dolled up in a white dress and strutting down that aisle in my direction.

I didn't want a wife or a girlfriend. I was already in a long-term relationship with the game I loved so much. And I wasn't about to mess that up to raise someone's brat. Even if that brat happened to share some of my DNA.

"And I'm just supposed to take your word for it?" she countered.

"I took yours, didn't I? When you sat down at my table and stamped a price tag on this sweet little cunt of yours." I trailed a hand between us, swiping a finger through the juices collecting on her clit before lifting it to my mouth and sucking it clean. "It's funny that you actually think I'd let anything separate me from slicing through a nice piece of virgin pussy."

"I needed the money," she whispered, barely loud enough for me to hear her.

"We all need something, baby girl." I grinned. "It's what makes the world go round. Supply and demand, a little *tit* for tat." I moved my hand up and pinched one of her nipples between my thumb and index finger for emphasis. "It's an exchange of goods. Like you said, you needed the money. And, well, lucky for you, I needed to release the tension of a long day. That's called fair trade."

"It's not a trade when I go home empty-handed."

I pressed a finger to her lips, just hard enough to exact a twinge of pain as I leaned forward until there was barely a breath separating us. "You'll go home debt free and fully satisfied. Which far surpasses the terms of our little agreement."

I was losing my patience now. I didn't appreciate back-talk. Not when there were far better uses for that smart mouth of hers. I pinched her cheeks together before pushing off the bed and rising to my full height, my cocked primed and at the ready. Just waiting to sink into whatever warm hole was prepared to take it. There were different types of virginity after all. Pussy was just the one I preferred over the rest.

I crooked a finger in the girl's direction. "Come here." Once again, it wasn't a request. It was a command. "On your knees. In front of me." I waited for her to scurry off the bed and do as she was told, glaring down at her as I asked the question presently bouncing around inside my mind. "You ever sucked a cock before?"

CHAPTER EIGHT

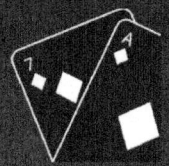

The girl shook her head. I could see the panic rising in her chest, her labored breaths more indicative of fear than the mounting pleasure I'd already offered her. It didn't matter. I could work with either. And I enjoyed the look of both.

I grabbed her chin, gently stroking my thumb over her jawline as I forced her eyes to meet mine. "Then it's about time someone teaches you, baby girl."

I could feel her swallow beneath my grip and could already imagine her drinking down so much more. My cock twitched at the thought, imagining what it would feel like to be jammed so far down that throat of hers it was hard to breathe. For her. Not me. I was breathing just fine.

The fantasy was good. But the reality was always so much better.

It took the slightest bit of pressure to pry her mouth open. Just wide enough to take the width of me as I fisted my cock at the base and eased it forward. For my own benefit and not hers. Having to knock someone's teeth out was not on my list of kinks. And I wasn't sure I could control myself if the girl got frisky and decided to bite down. Just another reason I wasn't as keen on getting sucked off by a stranger. There was a shit-ton of trust involved. And the only person I trusted was *me*.

I slowly inched myself forward, her lips curling with the action as I continued to rub the pad of my thumb over the soft skin of her throat. Coaxing her muscles into a more relaxed state while her eyes watered at the corners and her nostrils flared. Shit was uncomfortable, I was sure. And it was about to feel a whole lot worse.

I thrusted in as far as I could go without forcing her breakfast up the wrong way before pulling back and repeating the process. Her mouth was warm and perfectly wet. But it was clear the girl didn't know what to do with her tongue. Whether she should flatten it and tuck it out of the way or use it to lap at my cock like a lollipop.

It was fine though. My favorite part was teaching them anyway. Showing them what I liked while getting myself off.

Whenever her jaw would start to tighten, her teeth dangerously close to leaving imprints, I'd press my thumb on her jugular. Forcing her to slacken her muscles and swallow to ease the discomfort. It was another careful dance, but this time it only took my little molly a couple of minutes to learn the steps.

After a few back-and-forth motions—my cock properly slathered in her saliva, my hand now wrapped around a fistful of her hair, and her gagging sounds bouncing off the walls—I could feel myself edging closer and closer to the point of no return. My balls constricted as that familiar tingle traveled up the base of my spine and down again.

I tugged her head back, driving my cock deeper into her curved throat as those honeyed eyes seared into mine, and I came until her cheeks were puffing out at the sides. Her pursed lips keeping me in place as I struggled to stay upright.

I was lightheaded, drunk on the sudden surge of endorphins flooding my system as a smirk tipped up one side of my face.

If her throat was this good, I could only imagine what her cunt would feel like.

I shoved that thought aside as my glare dropped to those plump peach-like cheeks she was currently balancing on the balls of her feet—when they should be bouncing against my dick—as she did her best to keep herself from tipping over.

And then my mouth broke out into a full-on

grin. *Her pussy would have to wait, seeing as the next item on the menu was that sweet little ass.*

CHAPTER NINE

"Bend over." I didn't wait for the girl to reply before I was tugging her to her feet and pushing her face against the mattress. Her ass in the air and her cunt at eye level as I dropped to my knees and licked her from hole to hole.

I could hear her muffled panic when she tried to lift her head, only to have me reach up an arm and shove her down again. Not all women liked having their starfish eaten out but you never knew until you tried. And she sure as shit wasn't gonna enjoy me fucking her there if I didn't lube her up first.

I circled my tongue around her little puckered hole, flicking and sucking a few times before snaking it forward. She was clenching her muscles when what I needed was for her to relax. So I pushed to my feet and leaned over, my cock knocking against her backdoor as I whispered in her ear.

"You ever been fucked here before, baby girl?" I rotated my hips in a circular motion, precum marking each of her cheeks just in case there was any kind of... *misunderstanding* about which *here* I was talking about. Of course, I already knew the answer. But I liked to hear them say it.

She swallowed once. Her anxiety so heightened I could feel it vibrate across her pebbled skin. "I... no..." She shook her head from side to side, and I lowered my mouth again and nipped at her ear.

"Good. Another first," I grunted as I pushed back off the mattress and crouched behind her. "I'm gonna need you to relax, though. Or this one's really gonna burn."

This time, she gasped when I started lapping at her asshole—probably a mix of shock and the sensation of the warmth of my mouth warring with the cool breath I blew over her afterwards. If she was more focused on everything *she was feeling*, she was less likely to think too hard about what *I was doing*.

I continued eating away at her ass, as my thumb slinked around her waist and rubbed at her clit. The sounds I was making were obnoxious. Wet and sloppy. While the sounds she was making were soft and guttural. Little whimpers and moans that told me she hated how much she liked what I was doing to her.

By the time her next orgasm hit her, she was too dazed to do much else but lie there. Her face still buried in the sheets as I grabbed a bottle of lube from the dresser, poured a healthy portion into my palm, and stroked myself. Once, twice. Then twice more before I stopped. If I kept going, I was gonna come just watching her.

She looked so pretty, ass up and cunt out. My saliva dripping from both as I closed the distance and gave her a solid slap to the cheek to get her blood flowing again. The sudden sting of flesh on flesh had her bolting upright at the same time I pressed myself behind her, my cock already inching into the next hole it was gonna claim tonight.

CHAPTER TEN

Once you got past the tip, the burn wasn't so bad. At least from what I could tell. They usually stopped crying by that point. And I don't mean full-on sobbing. I wasn't an asshole. Just currently fucking one as a few tears formed at the corners of her eyes.

Shit was painful. I had no doubt about that. But with that came the pleasure of me coming at her from both sides, my thumb on her clit and my dick in her ass, so that she was locked between two different sensations that somehow worked together to stimulate nerve endings she didn't even know she had. Because as much as she bucked against me at first, she leaned into me now. Meeting me thrust for thrust. Her hair wild, back arched, and thighs trembling.

I closed my eyes as the sweat beaded over my

forehead before dripping onto my nose. Dropping my hands to the curve of her waist and forcing her against the mattress again. My orgasm was close, her next one was closer if the rhythm of her breaths was anything to go by.

I knew the moment it hit her. She'd had enough of them tonight that I recognized the way her body went limp. How the shivers traveled across her skin and had her convulsing before she went perfectly still. A tiny sigh would part her lips until one side of her mouth tipped up into the makings of a smirk. Like a kid whose hand had been caught in the cookie jar.

Another slap to her ass had her jerking backwards as I tugged her closer, my fist wrapped around her hair, and rode out my own orgasm. I couldn't describe the feeling if I wanted to. No words seemed right when it came to explaining how those rings of muscles clenched around you almost like they were trying to hold you in place. Like they were in a fight for their life and strangling your cock was the only way to survive. Like your soul left your body the moment your cum did the same thing.

An extended orgasm was God's gift to mankind. I had no doubt about that as two more spirts exited my tip and splattered across the girl's back. I reached out a hand and drew a little heart with my fingertip —it was my favorite suit. *The queen of hearts knew how to treat a guy.* Then I pivoted on my heel and went in search of a towel.

Had to clean myself up if I planned on fucking her cunt next. And there was no denying that that was exactly what I was gonna do *next*. It was the last item on my checklist. The last thing we were gonna share together before we never saw each other again.

Unless this little molly was dumb enough to try her hand at another round of poker at one of my tables. Could only hope she had enough cash on her if she did, though. Seeing as she was one hole shy of having nothing left to offer me anymore.

CHAPTER ELEVEN

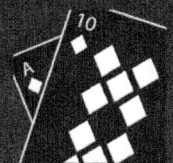

Pussy was a living, breathing organism of its own. Each had a unique scent, flavor... *elasticity*. Like a snowflake or flower petal or brush stroke. And I indulged in all of them. The shape or size didn't matter as long as I was the first one to tear into the packaging. And this girl's was as much the same as it was different somehow.

I couldn't put my finger on it—*excuse the choice of words... or don't*. But something about the way she stared up at me from where I now had her sprawled out on the bedsheets, my cum barely dried on her lips and back, had my cock hard all over again. There was the innocence I enjoyed, of course. The inquisitiveness that came with doing something she knew she shouldn't. But there was also a hint of defiance. A need to both comply and disobey warring with each other beneath the surface.

She liked to be my good little girl at the same time some deeper part of her was dying to be my perfect little slut instead.

That was new, and I couldn't help but wonder what she did in her bedroom, late at night, when no one was watching. Did she fantasize about a man like me climbing through her window and taking her in her sleep? Was her virginity as much of a burden as it was my prize? And why the fuck did I care?

I didn't. I was just curious. The girl had piqued my interests the moment she sat at my table and lifted a challenging brow in my direction. She was asking for trouble and she'd found it.

But that wasn't all she found. She found pleasure too. Hours and hours of thigh-quivering pleasure.

The moment my hand drifted from the curve of her waist, over her soft thigh before brushing along her cunt—wet and fluttering with need—I had to remind myself this was a marathon and not a race. The finish line signaled the end of our evening and I just wasn't ready to step on the platform and hold that trophy over my head.

No, I wasn't ready for the experience to be over yet.

She squirmed beneath my hold, no matter how soft or hard I teased at her swollen clit. She was over-stimulated, her pretty pink nipples stiffened to peaks that were just begging to be squeezed and twisted. Licked and sucked.

I bent forward, keeping my body weight trained on one arm as I closed my mouth over the flesh of her left breast while my free hand continued to stroke and torment. She was a wanton little thing now that she'd experienced her first few orgasms, her whimpers just barely audible as she tried to bite her lower lip and keep them in.

Thing was, they weren't hers to keep. They were mine. I'd earned them and I wanted to hear them. I wanted to hear all the sounds I could compel her to make with just a simple twirl of my finger, nip of my teeth, lap of my tongue.

I stilled my movements, gliding my hand back up the length of her body until it reached her chin. Grabbed her jaw and pried it open. "If I wanted to fuck a church mouse, I would have joined the priesthood, sweetheart," I grunted, and waited for my meaning to sink in.

It didn't take long. Girl might have been a shit poker player but there was more than air upstairs. She was sharp and eager to please. Which meant she was teachable. *Thank fuck.*

The little moans she was making grew louder but not too loud. As much as I didn't want that church mouse, I didn't want a porn star either. Or a performance. I didn't want anything I didn't deserve. I didn't count cards or cheat my way to the pot. It wasn't about inflating my ego. I was self-aware enough to know I had flaws. This just wasn't one of them. I was good at what I did at both the table and in the bedroom. Everyone was gifted with certain abilities, indulged in certain vices. Pussy and poker were mine.

CHAPTER TWELVE

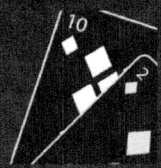

I could hear the clock ticking in the background, reminding me that how we started was very much how we were gonna end. This Cinderella had an expiration date and she was one deep thrust away from turning into a pumpkin—it wasn't my fault I just so happened to prefer my fruit... *unseeded.*

I pushed myself up on my knees, her thighs butterflied open around me as I grabbed each of her ankles and dragged her down the mattress. Closer. Nothing was better than watching the head of my cock glide forward and disappear between a set of puffy pussy lips. It was my favorite part. That initial penetration that both endeared the girl *to me* and ruined her *for me.*

Her abdominal muscles rose and fell with her quickened breaths, as I used my thumb to spread her open. Notched my cock at her entrance and braced myself for that first rush of adrenaline. The same one I felt every time I stepped away from a table with more zeroes in my bank account than I started with.

I could feel the warmth flooding my system, the same time a different kind of warmth flooded my cock. I'd spent the last few hours ensuring her body was ready for me, that the resistance was just enough to grip me from all sides without taking a layer of skin off my dick. Like I said, her pleasure was as much about me as it was about her. Tight, virgin pussies were a luxury... but they could also be painful as fuck. And that just wasn't my thing.

Though it might have been hers if the look on her face the moment I broke through the last barrier separating us was anything to go by. Her body tensed before it melted against the sheets like a deflated balloon. Just as still and shapeless. Until I pulled back and thrusted forward again.

Her hands clawed at the sheets, her legs shaky as I leveraged them against my hips, tugging her ass up each time I drove down. She was a slight thing but that didn't mean her cheeks didn't clap in rhythm with my thrusts. Just audible over the sound of her moans mixing with my own labored breaths.

My abdominal muscles screamed and my biceps ached before I gave up on fighting gravity, tucked her left leg around my waist and dropped onto my thighs. Which had the entire bedframe shaking now, the headboard thudding against the wall hard enough to leave marks. She scrambled to grab my face, drawing it closer as I shoved my tongue down her throat, forcing her to taste herself as much as she could taste me.

She might not have liked me, but she sure as fuck liked what I did to her.

Three more slow pumps, combined with a circular motion that had my pelvic bone grinding against her clit, had her seeing stars again. She sighed into my mouth before prying her lips free and dropping her head back against the mattress. I could almost make out the whites of her eyes as she clung to the headboard and arched her back against me.

There was nothing quite like your first internal orgasm. I might not have been able to experience it directly, but I didn't have to. Not when I could witness it this up close and personal. Just watching her—the way her mouth remained slightly parted, her hair wild and unkempt, her cheeks flush, and her nostrils flared—was enough to send that first spirt of cum deep inside her cunt. Then another and another, until I could barely hold myself upright to stop from crushing her.

CHAPTER THIRTEEN

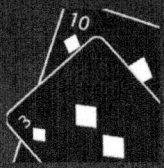

It was the same every time. The immediate low that followed the highest of highs. My heart beat evened out, my blood pressure dropped —along with the thrill—and then I was left with that familiar emptiness. The one that had me in a chokehold until the next time I entered a room, took my usual spot at the table, and had the first hand of cards thrown out in front of me. Until I holed myself up in my usual suite and made good use of the bleach-white sheets.

I looked up at my reflection in the mirror before chancing a glance over the shoulder at the girl still curled up in my bed. She was such a slight thing I could just make out the shape of her body from here.

That was a problem.

The only thing I avoided more than repeat

offenders was slumber parties. Which meant my little pillow princess had to go.

I slammed the bathroom door closed, loud enough that it would wake her if she was in fact sleeping and not just faking it. Turned the tap on the coldest setting and splashed some water on my face before tucking a fresh towel around my waist. What I wanted was a hot shower, something to soothe the sore muscles that told me my night had been well spent. But what I *needed* was help ensuring this girl didn't make a scene when I threw her ass out. Not that I couldn't handle her on my own. I just didn't care to. Especially when I had more than enough cash to pay someone else to do it for me.

I reached out an arm and swiped up the phone that was mounted to the wall to my right. The concierge answered on the second ring, which told me he hadn't been sitting at his desk and had to make a quick dash for it. Hospitality knew I didn't like waiting—*as a long-term guest, I shouldn't have had to.*

"Good evening, Mr. Bettencourt, how may we assist you?" an older man hummed down the line, sounding a little too chipper at this time of night— my eyes flicked to the gold watch I hadn't bothered to remove—or should I say morning? It was already half-past three.

"I have a guest who needs help finding the front door," I grunted into the receiver. I didn't have to say more. The staff knew what was expected of them and security had certain measures in place if things got a little... hairy. It was amazing what a few extra hundred-dollar bills shoved into someone's palm could do for you. How quickly a stiff set of morals could be pushed aside and forgotten about.

I listened to the sound of tapping on a keyboard in the background before the concierge's voice whispered down the line again, "The woman in the green dress?" He'd been pulling up the security footage, preparing to delete it—as was protocol—until something must have stopped him.

"Yes. Why? Is there a problem?" It wasn't really a question. It was a latent threat. I didn't care if this girl was this fucker's granddaughter. I paid him to turn a blind eye, and that's exactly what he was gonna do. Or he would be heading out the door right along with her.

There was a long pause, my irritation growing in tandem with the rapid clicking sounds and the quick shuffling of steps. And then I heard the pounding of boots. Security, I could only assume.

"I said is there a fucking problem?" I barked between clenched teeth.

"Is she there with you now, sir?" he asked, his voice a little shakier than it was a moment ago.

"Who? The girl?" I couldn't stop myself from glancing over a shoulder again, even though there was still a door between us. "She's in the other room.

Why? What the fuck is going on?" By the time I swung it back open, stretching the phone cord as I stepped out of the en suite and into the main living space, security was forcing their way inside.

"You may want to check for your wallet, sir." The breeze from the now-open window left my towel fluttering, chilling my balls while the concierge's words sent a similar chill down my spine. "According to the pit manager, it's the fifth time that girl's *lost her virginity* this week."

CHAPTER FOURTEEN

I glanced out the window as the streets continued to blur by, the light rain clinging to the glass and giving the outside world a distorted appearance. So that everything looked like blobs of different colors and shapes. It was somehow both pretty and grotesque at the same time. Kind of like the man who was smart enough to clean house at the table every night, but too dumb to keep an eye on his winnings when there was a stranger in his bed.

The rumors were true. I'd give him that, though. That tongue of his knew how to work wonders. It was just a shame it was still attached to the rest of him.

I let out a loud sigh before righting myself in my seat as I drew the ace of diamonds from the hidden pocket in my sleeve. The same card that could have earned me my winnings at the table, instead of at the expense of my opponent's pride. But the satisfied throb between my legs told me that once again, I'd made the right choice by staying in the game until I was able to take the entire pot.

"Where to, Miss?" The older gentleman tapped on the steering wheel while staring at me through the rear-view mirror. He had kind eyes, the sort that were circled by little crow's feet that deepened with his laugh lines when he smiled at me. That smile would earn the man a hefty tip this morning.

I guess you could say I was a little like Robin Hood when it came to how I treated people—rob from the rich and give to the poor and all that.

"The Venetian, please," I replied, using my most polite tone—just like my mama taught me—as my eyes dropped to the compact in my hand. I quickly reapplied my favorite shade of lipstick before flitting my gaze back up to the cab driver.

"Spending the night?" he mused.

My lips, now several hues darker, curled while my perfectly manicured eyebrow arched with the challenge. "No, but I hear they have a killer card table?"

EPILOGUE

Sometime later. How long?
Long enough for our girl to get bored
all over again.

I tapped the back of my nail against the table —*it was a sign of annoyance.* And not a tell. I didn't have any tells. What I did have was another winning hand.

I didn't have to see the other side of their cards to know tonight's crowd was choking on more than the tobacco that darkened their lungs. I loved poker, but I hated the stench of cigar smoke that came with it. Almost like these assholes didn't know how to play the game without a cancer stick shoved between their lips. Or maybe it had more to do with an oral fixation.

In that case, I'd give them something to suck on.

I flicked my eyes up at the man sitting across from me, over the yellowing of his teeth and the crumbs that had made a nest in his beard.

Or maybe not.

The image of letting that mouth anywhere near my lady parts had my pussy clamping shut and closing up shop. Not that she had any customers currently trying to knock the door down.

I slammed my strawberry daiquiri onto the table at the thought. And immediately regretted it. It wasn't the bartender's fault I was wound so tight. It was mine. Sorta.

I guess you could say I was having a bit of a dry spell, and it had nothing to do with how much cash I was raking in every night and everything to do with the fact I hadn't been properly fucked since the last time I wore this green dress. I didn't wear the same thing twice, and not because I was wasteful. It was just smarter to change things up. Eye color, hair color, sometimes height—*finally found a good use for those god-awful six-inch heels, even if I risked an ankle with each step I took in them.*

Today, I'd broken that rule. Call me superstitious, but I thought this dress might bring me a little luck. Instead, all I was getting was a headache and a pair of singed eyebrows.

I didn't look up when a figure darkened the seat next to mine. I didn't need to. The men here were all the same. Old, married, creepy. With the kind of bloodshot eyes that leered much longer than was polite whenever I leaned over the table to toss in another chip. Couldn't fault them though. I had nice... *assets*. The sort that kept the male gaze from focusing too hard on my sleight of hand.

I didn't cheat to win. I didn't have to. I just let the game play out a little longer when the pot was too small, the table too empty—or let's be honest, when I was just plain bored and wanted to fuck with someone. Kind of like right now.

"I wouldn't do that if I were you... Rosalind," a deep, baritone voice whispered next to my ear the moment my fingertips danced over the card I planned to tuck into my sleeve.

I'd never been caught before, but that didn't mean I hadn't thought about what I would do if I ever found myself in this predicament. Besides, I enjoyed improvising. There was a certain thrill that came with it.

Which was why I still didn't bother looking up as those same fingertips dropped from the card in my sleeve and trailed up the stranger's thigh. He knew my name. Which I admit was a little unnerving. Then again, a quick glance at the ID I had to use to sign in could have told him that.

"I'm sorry. Do I know you?" I asked as my gaze danced over the custom stitching of his suit, the gold buttons of his jacket, and the crisp seams of his dress shirt before landing on a jaw that was so sharp and tense it could cut a girl's pussy in two.

"Do you know me?" he hissed. "I would like to think so... Perhaps the wallet you stole would help jar that shit memory of yours?"

"Oh, yeah, I *remember* you now." I grinned, grabbing onto the guy's jacket and smoothing out the slight wrinkle in his lapel.

His arm snapped out before his palm quickly closed around my wrist. Keeping me just out of reach and halting my movements. He didn't trust me. I couldn't blame him. I didn't trust me either. Especially right now.

"But the way I see it... I didn't steal shit, Mr. Bettencourt. I simply took what was owed to me after I *sold* ya my V-card. Would you like to buy it again?"

FROM THE AUTHOR

THE MORAL OF THE STORY IS:
NO ONE CAN TAKE YOUR V-CARD
BUT YOU SURE AS SHIT CAN GIVE IT AWAY...
AS MANY TIMES AS YOU'D LIKE.
JUST ASK ROSALIND.

◆♠♥♣◆♣♥♠◆

ACKNOWLEDGMENTS

THANKS TO EVERYONE WHO HAS BEEN A PART OF THIS LONG-ASS PROCESS. TO EVERYONE WHO HAS SHARED, LIKED, COMMENTED, AND PREORDERED. TO THOSE OF YOU WHO TOOK A CHANCE ON ME AND MY FUCKED-UP BRAIN.

I COULD NOT HAVE DONE IT WITHOUT YOU, AND I AM SO VERY HUMBLED.

I ALSO WANTED TO SAY THANK YOU TO MY ARC READERS, WHO ARE TAKING TIME OUT OF THEIR BUSY SCHEDULES TO READ AND REVIEW MY BOOK. AND THANK YOU TO THOSE OF YOU WHO WENT AS FAR AS TO READ AND REVIEW MY PRIOR PUBLICATIONS TOO—I SEE YOU AND I AM SO GRATEFUL FOR YOU.

◆♠♥♣◆♠♥♣◆

ALSO BY SYBIL KNIGHT

THE TRUTH AND LIES DUET:

The Harsher the Truth

The Sweeter the Lies

THE RENEGADES SERIES:

Skin

Lamb

Bells

STANDALONE NOVELS:

Half Cocked

Kill Joy

STANDALONE NOVELLAS:

SINS OF OUR FATHERS

V CARD

I'LL BE SEEING YOU

THE MORE THE MERRIER

EAT YOUR HEART OUT

MORE TITLES TO COME...

♦♠♥♣♦♠♥♣♦

ABOUT THE AUTHOR

Sybil is a career-driven Philadelphian native. A crime show enthusiast by day, and a BDSM club hopper by night. When she isn't working or writing, she is talking about working or writing. She is a single mom to her betta fish (Fish) and way too many dead houseplants.

Her stories range from gray to black, with darker themes throughout. She prefers heroines with a kick-ass mentality and the heroes who know how to rein them in. The mental and medical aspects of her books are well-researched, though they are given a humanistic approach and diagnoses aren't the focal points. She believes her characters don't need to wear labels in order to get their messages across.

Her books are mostly standalones, though her characters may interact and intersect worlds. Additionally, she works closely with and writes alongside author Dahlia Reign and some characters will appear in cameos in each of their publications.

Sybil welcomes emails from readers if there are concerns or questions regarding any of her publications.

Email: AUTHORSYBILKNIGHT@GMAIL.COM

Printed in Dunstable, United Kingdom